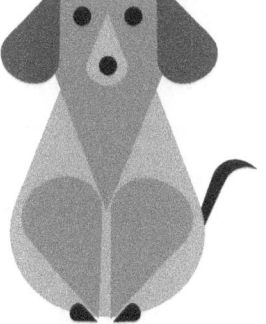

pinpoint ENGLISH
whole class reading

Flexible and Creative Lessons for

The Explorer

by Katherine Rundell

Y5

Published by Pearson Education Limited, 80 Strand, London, WC2R 0RL.

www.pearsonschools.co.uk

Text © Pearson Education Limited 2019
Edited by Pearson Education Limited and Just Content Limited
Designed and typeset by Pearson Education Limited and PDQ Media
Original illustrations © Pearson Education Limited 2019
Illustrated by PDQ Media
Characters illustrated by The Boy Fitz Hammond
Cover design by Pearson
Cover illustration © Pearson Education Limited 2019

The right of Sarah Loader to be identified as author of this work has been asserted by her in accordance with the Copyright, Designs and Patents Act 1988.

First published 2019

22 21 20 19
10 9 8 7 6 5 4 3 2 1

British Library Cataloguing in Publication Data
A catalogue record for this book is available from the British Library

ISBN 978 1 292 27395 2

Copyright notice
All rights reserved. The material in this publication is copyright. Activity sheets may be freely photocopied for classroom use in the purchasing institution. However, this material is copyright and under no circumstances may copies be offered for sale. If you wish to use the material in any way other than that specified you must apply in writing to the publishers.

Printed in the UK by Ashford Press Ltd

Acknowledgements

P60: The Road-Song of the Bandar-Log, poem in *The Jungle Book, by Rudyard Kipling*, © 1894, Rudyard Kipling;
P61: Letting in the Jungle, story in *The Second Jungle Book, by Rudyard Kipling*, © 1895, Rudyard Kipling;
P62–63: The Law of the Jungle, poem in *The Second Jungle Book, by Rudyard Kipling*, © 1895, Rudyard Kipling.

Note from the publisher
Pearson has robust editorial processes, including answer and fact checks, to ensure the accuracy of the content in this publication, and every effort is made to ensure this publication is free of errors. We are, however, only human, and occasionally errors do occur. Pearson is not liable for any misunderstandings that arise as a result of errors in this publication, but it is our priority to ensure that the content is accurate. If you spot an error, please do contact us at resourcescorrections@pearson.com so we can make sure it is corrected.

Contents

Programme overview	4
Using Whole Class Reading	5
Activity planning guide	6
Synopsis	8
Starter activities	9
Main activities	21
Plenary activities	36
Photocopy masters	50
Answers	64

Programme overview

Introduction

Pinpoint English Whole Class Reading is your new go-to resource for flexible, high-quality activities based on the best children's books, with a strong focus on turning readers into writers and developing rich vocabularies.

Whole Class Reading is curriculum-matched, allowing you to target the skills required to ensure success in the national curriculum for English.

Principles

- As the teacher, you can choose which texts to teach in which order, matching with your focus topic for a particular week or term, the needs of your class or just your personal favourites.
- Each text has been chosen by an experienced panel of children's writers, librarians and teachers.
- The Whole Class Reading series allows you to rediscover classroom favourites as well as explore new titles that champion diversity and broaden your class's horizons.
- Activities provide opportunities to engage with fiction, poetry and non-fiction, with curriculum objectives provided for each task.
- Reading comprehension is taught through discussion and written activities, providing practice of essential skills.
- Spoken language skills are improved through lively debate, discussions and games.
- Vocabulary, spelling and grammar are taught in the context of a real writer's choices.
- Activities are differentiated where appropriate yet complementary so that the whole class can enjoy reading together.

Programme structure

- Whole Class Reading provides a vast, flexible range of starter, main and plenary activities to empower you to teach with confidence.
- Review the activities, pinpoint the skills you want to cover and build engaging lessons.
- Look out for differentiated activities to allow you to keep the whole class together.

 These tasks provide a low-threshold starting point to build the foundations of understanding.

 These tasks are pitched at age-related expectations so that children who can complete the work confidently and accurately display a firm grasp of the topic or skill.

 These tasks challenge children to explore the topic or skill in greater depth.

Using Whole Class Reading

> Suggested **activity timings** are shown here. Some activities can be carried out over several lessons.

> **Resource lists** let you know which photocopy masters and materials you will need.

> **Milestones** suggest how far you should read before carrying out the activity.

> **Vocabulary builder** activities help your class to expand their vocabularies.

Poetry: Write a poem

(10) (WORD) vocabulary builder **Resources required:** photocopy master (PCM) 10 (T only)

(AFTER READING)

- **Children should be able to:**
  - identify the audience for and purpose of the writing; select appropriate grammar and vocabulary.
  - prepare poems to read aloud and to perform.

1 Explain to the class that they're going to write their own short poem about *The Explorer*, and that the poem can be written about, or in response to, any element of the book: an event; a character; a friendship; an animal; a sight or sound, etc.

2 Explain to the class that poems don't have to rhyme, but they should be evocative and powerful in representing something from the book.

3 Children could read their poems out once they're finished.

(T) Ask children to look at PCM 10 for support.

—— Plenary activity 27

> Each activity explores areas of the **national curriculum**.

> The main activity steps are pitched at the 'Securing' level. Where appropriate, you will find **differentiation ideas** here.

Curriculum areas covered in this title

- spoken language
- reading
- writing
- spelling, punctuation and grammar
- citizenship
- physical education
- history
- design and technology
- mathematics
- science
- geography
- art and design

Activity planning guide

The magic of Whole Class Reading is that you can mix and match activities in a way that works for you, your class and the time you can dedicate to *The Explorer*. Sometimes, you might spend a whole lesson reading; at other times, you might build a structured lesson from the 90 activities you'll find in this book. Below is an overview of these activities, complete with reading milestones (in brackets) and pairing suggestions.

Starter activities

1: *Speaking* (before reading)
Predict what might happen.

2: *Citizenship* (during reading)
Try some Brazilian foods.
Works well with Plenary 2.

3: *Speaking; reading* (to page 7)
Predict what happens next.

4: *Speaking; reading* (to page 165)
Predict what happens next.

5: *Speaking; reading* (to page 335)
Predict what happens next.

6: *Speaking; reading* (to page 385)
Predict what happens next.

7: *Speaking* (to page 7)
Debate which items are important.

8: *Speaking* (to page 32)
Interview a character.

9: *Speaking* (to page 138)
Interview a character.

10: *Speaking* (to page 176)
Interview a character.

11: *Speaking* (to page 203)
Interview a character.

12: *Speaking* (to page 225)
Interview a character.

13: *Speaking* (to page 342)
Interview a character.

14: *Speaking* (to page 394)
Interview a character.

15: *Speaking* (to page 162)
Consider the children's qualities to choose a leader for the group.

16: *Vocabulary* (to page 169)
Describe sights, sounds and smells.

Main activities

1: *Writing* (to page 12)
Write alternative openings.

2–5: *Design and technology* (to page 76)
Design and build a model raft, before testing its ability to float. This is a four-lesson mini-project.

6: *Writing* (during reading)
Write alternative endings based on key decisions.

7: *Geography* (to page 138)
Draw a map of a familiar place.

8: *Writing* (to page 185)
Write a letter home from one of the characters.

9: *Writing* (to page 203)
Write in the explorer's diary.

10: *Writing* (to page 225)
Write in the explorer's diary.

11: *Writing* (to page 309)
Write in the explorer's diary.

12: *Writing* (to page 376)
Write in the explorer's diary.

13: *Art* (to page 315)
Use symbolism to design a tattoo.
Works well with Starter 20.

14: *Writing* (after reading)
Write an Amazon survival guide.

15: *Writing* (after reading)
Imagine letters between the characters as grown-ups.

16: *Writing* (after reading)
Write an autobiography from one of the characters' perspectives.

Plenary activities

1: *Writing; grammar* (to page 7)
Work with fronted adverbials.

2: *Writing* (during reading)
Write reviews for Brazilian foods.
Works well with Starter 2.

3: *Vocabulary* (to page 83)
Bring things to life using language.

4: *Vocabulary* (during reading)
Explore unknown vocabulary.

5: *Reading* (to page 176)
Order activities from the book.

6: *Reading* (to page 315)
Order activities from the book.

7: *Reading* (after reading)
Order activities from the book.

8: *Vocabulary* (to page 200)
Search for answers to the quiz.

9: *Vocabulary* (to page 331)
Search for answers to the quiz.

10: *Vocabulary* (to page 375)
Search for answers to the quiz.

11: *Writing* (to page 138)
Write directions to a familiar place.

12: *Vocabulary* (to page 304)
Use imaginative language to describe family members.

13: *PE* (to page 328)
Play a game of stuck in the mud.

14: *Speaking* (to page 333)
Discuss an important memory.

15: *Vocabulary* (to page 373)
Create exciting metaphors.

Starter activities

17: *Vocabulary* (to page 292)
Describe sights, sounds and smells.

18: *Vocabulary* (to page 359)
Describe sights, sounds and smells.

19: *Speaking* (to page 225)
Debate whether the ruined city should be kept a secret.

20: *Citizenship* (to page 315)
Explore how symbols reflect beliefs and show belonging.
Works well with Main 13.

21: *Speaking* (after reading)
Hold imaginary job interviews for the characters.
Works well with Plenary 18.

22: *Drama* (after reading)
Create freeze frames.

23: *Speaking* (after reading)
Discuss favourite moments from the book.

24: *Drama* (after reading)
Play charades, acting out key scenes from the book.

25: *Speaking* (after reading)
Pitch the book to Hollywood.
Works well with Plenary 20.

26: *Speaking* (after reading)
Create dangerous animal cards.

27: *PE* (after reading)
Play the traditional Mayan game of pok-a-tok.
Can be played frequently.

28: *Speaking* (after reading)
Play the dangerous animal game.
Pre-requisite: Starter 26. Can be played frequently.

29: *Speaking* (after reading)
Debate which character from the book would win the final place at the dinner table.

30: *Vocabulary* (after reading)
Find imaginative synonyms.
Works well with Main 30 and Plenary 27.

Main activities

17–19: *Geography; writing* (after reading)
Report on the threats to the Amazon rainforest.
This is a three-lesson mini-project.

20: *Writing; art* (after reading)
Create an Amazon cookbook.

21: *Writing; reading* (after reading)
Write true or false quizzes.
Quizzes used in Plenary 21.

22: *Writing* (after reading)
Write a prequel about the explorer.

23–25: *Writing; history; geography* (after reading)
Learn about and report on the Ancient Mayans.
This is a three-lesson mini-project.

26–28: *Writing; geography* (after reading)
Create a travel documentary about South America.
This is a two-lesson mini-project.

28: *Writing* (after reading)
Write a newspaper article.

29: *Writing* (after reading)
Write instructions for a new game.

30: *Reading; speaking* (after reading)
Explore and perform poems.
Works well with Starter 30 and Plenary 27.

Plenary activities

16: *Speaking* (to page 381)
Discuss bravery and personal achievements.

17: *Vocabulary* (to page 388)
Explore definitions of 'exploring'.

18: *Writing* (to page 394)
Write a CV for a character.
Works well with Starter 21.

19: *Writing* (after reading)
Write an honest character summary of yourself.

20: *Speaking* (after reading)
Decide which members of the class could play each character in a film.
Works well with Starter 25.

21: *Reading* (after reading)
Complete true or false quizzes.
Prerequisite: Main 21.

22: *Writing* (after reading)
Write a sequel to *The Explorer*.

23: *Writing* (after reading)
Write newspaper headlines.

24: *Writing* (after reading)
Create an Amazon animal fact file.

25: *Writing* (after reading)
Write a 'before' school report for one of the characters.
Use before Plenary 26.

26: *Writing* (after reading)
Write an 'after' school report for one of the characters.
Use after Plenary 25.

27: *Writing* (after reading)
Write a poem about *The Explorer*.
Works well with Main 30 and Plenary 27.

28: *Drama* (after reading)
Record a trailer for *The Explorer*.

29: *Geography* (after reading)
Compare the UK and the Amazon.

30: *Speaking* (after reading)
Compile lists of characters' personality traits.

Synopsis

The Explorer by Katherine Rundell

When the plane carrying four children across the Amazon jungle towards Manaus crashes, their lives change forever. Stranded in the jungle with no other survivors and nothing but the clothes they're wearing, Fred, Con, Lila and Max embark on the adventure of their lives in a bid for survival and, ultimately, a route out of the jungle and back home.

The camp the children set up is fine for a while, but it's a struggle to find food and the children know that they need to start moving or risk dying of starvation. Following the Amazon river into Manaus seems like the most sensible plan but they have no idea which direction to head in or how long their handmade raft will last. Plus, there's lots to be afraid of in the water – caiman, piranha – and while it's fine when the river's flat and calm, the children know that everything could change in a moment.

After a few days on the water, they come to a large lake and a steep cliff. Abandoning their raft, they climb to the top using the vines and are amazed when they stumble upon what looks like a ruined city and, even more amazingly, an explorer who lives there.

They never know his name, and he frightens them a bit, but the glimmers of kindness he shows the children and the knowledge that he could be their only real chance of survival forces them to stay and to try to befriend him.

As the children's unlikely friendship with the strange, elusive explorer develops, he teaches them how to live in the jungle. Their urgency to get home wanes and they begin to enjoy their new existence. Then everything changes. Max is attacked by bullet ants. They're deadly, and if the children don't get him to a hospital, he'll die very soon. Suddenly the children need the explorer more than ever, and the plane he has been hiding and working on for years comes into use. Flying the plane themselves, the children's final adventure begins. They fly out of the dense jungle towards Manaus, landing safely and saving Max's life. Finally, they are reunited with their families. We next meet them 12 years on and catch up on their stories of success as adults and their enduring, life-changing friendship.

About the author

Katherine Rundell is an award-winning author of four novels for children. She grew up in Africa and Europe, and travelled to the Amazon to research *The Explorer*. About the trip, she said, "I thought, before I went, that I knew what beauty was. I did not." She is particularly enthralled by the discovery of lost Mayan cities and the knowledge that there are, very likely, many more out there yet to be found: "The thought of it blows your hair back. There is still so much of the world to know." Rundell won the Waterstones Children's Book Prize and the Blue Peter Book Award for Best Story in 2014 for *Rooftoppers*. *The Explorer* was the Costa Children's Book of the Year in 2017.

Katherine grew up climbing trees and swimming, and nowadays enjoys tightrope and roof walking! Apparently she begins each day with a cartwheel because, as she says: "Reading is almost exactly the same as cartwheeling: it turns the world upside down and leaves you breathless."

Starter activities

Judge a book by its cover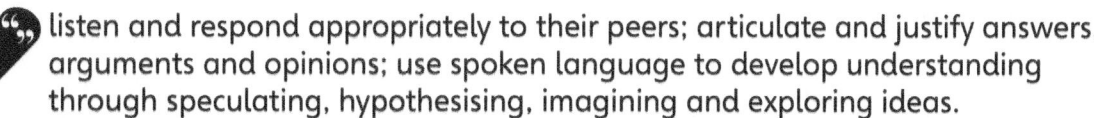

⏱ 5

- **Children should be able to:**

  💬 listen and respond appropriately to their peers; articulate and justify answers, arguments and opinions; use spoken language to develop understanding through speculating, hypothesising, imagining and exploring ideas.

  📖 predict what might happen from details stated and implied.

  ✏ select appropriate grammar and vocabulary.

1 Look together at the front cover of *The Explorer*. Ask children to express their ideas about the book: what it's about, where it's set and who might be in it.

2 Ask children to turn to page 1 and look at the illustration opposite the first chapter. Discuss whether this gives any further insight into the content of the book. What does it tell the class about the setting?

📍 Ask children to write a short blurb without reading the blurb on the back cover.

Starter activity 1

Taste of Brazil

⏱ 10 **Resources required:** a selection of Brazilian foods

- **Children should be able to:**

  👥 reflect on spiritual, moral, social and cultural issues, using imagination to understand other people's experiences; understand that difference and similarities between people arise from a number of factors, including cultural and ethnic diversity.

1 To set the scene in the jungle, buy or make some traditional Brazilian food for the class to try. Good examples include: Açai (hard purple berries); Pão de queijo (cheesy bread rolls); brigadeiros (chocolate truffles). Recipes for all these dishes are available online.

Alternatively, bring in some of the foods that the characters in the book eat while stranded in the Amazon – pineapple, honey, figs, cocoa beans – to give a flavour of their diet. Try these together as a class.

2 Ask the class to review the food as though they are judges in a cooking competition.

📍 Children could write reviews, comparing the food to more familiar cuisine.

This activity would work well with Plenary activity 2. Ensure you are familiar with any allergies in the class before this activity.

Starter activity 2

Predicting the future

DURING READING

4 × 5

- **Children should be able to:**

  listen and respond appropriately to their peers; articulate and justify answers, arguments and opinions; use spoken language to develop understanding through speculating, hypothesising, imagining and exploring ideas.

  predict what might happen from details stated and implied.

  indicate degrees of possibility using modal verbs.

1 Ask children to predict what will happen in the chapters below by reflecting on what has happened so far and using their imaginations.

  - *The Green Dark:* children can use the pictures on pages 6–7 for clues.
  - *On the River:* children can use the pictures on pages 164–165 for clues.
  - *Max:* children can use the pictures on pages 334–335 for clues.
  - *Another Kind of Exploring:* children can use the pictures on pages 384–385 for clues.

2 Encourage children to use modal verbs *(might, will, could, etc.)* to describe how likely or possible each part of their predictions are.

T Ask children to concentrate on events that might take place.

S Ask children to think about how characters might behave and feel in response to the events they are predicting.

D Ask children to think about the impact of the predicted events on characters' emotional resilience, and how they would cope with what might happen.

Starter activities 3–6

Group discussion: survival kit

- **Children should be able to:**

  listen and respond appropriately to adults and their peers; articulate and justify answers, arguments and opinions; consider and evaluate different viewpoints, attending to and building on the contributions of others.

1 List the following items on the board:
   - box of plasters
   - pocket mirror
   - small box of matches
   - bottle of water
   - pocket knife
   - tube of antiseptic cream
   - large plastic sheet
   - chocolate bar
   - piece of rope
   - mosquito net

   Explain that the children should imagine that they've just crash landed in the Amazon jungle. There are four of them and they are the only survivors. They have five minutes to gather supplies from the burning plane. They must decide, together, what they need most and least from the list on the board. They can only take eight items.

2 Divide the class into groups of four. Ask the groups to number the items from 1–8 in order of priority.

3 Each group takes turns to feed back to the rest of the class, explaining the reasons behind their priorities.

The groups should discuss and agree their decisions.

Starter activity 7

Role play

7 x

- **Children should be able to:**

   ask relevant questions to extend their understanding and knowledge; give well-structured descriptions, explanations and narratives for different purposes, including for expressing feelings; maintain attention and participate actively in collaborative conversations; participate in performances, role play and improvisations.

   infer characters' feelings, thought and motives.

1 Divide the class into pairs at the end of each of the chapters below. Each chapter ending marks the end of a section of significant character development. Explain that one child should go into role as an interviewer and the other as one of the characters.

2 Give the interviewers between five and ten minutes to interview their partners. Interviewers should ask questions that will delve into the personality of the character and what's just happened to them, to try to better understand them.

3 Ask children, in role as one of the characters, to think about how that character feels in relation to what's happening, how they feel about each other and what might have changed for them at each point.

- *The Den* (p 18–32); after the crash: character can be Fred, Con or Lila.
- *The Monkeys and the Bees* (p 114–138); finding the map: character can be Fred or Con.
- *On the River* (p 164–176); swimming with dolphins: character will be Fred.
- *The Ruined City* (p 186–203); at the ruined city: character can be Fred, Lila, Con or the explorer.
- *The Explorer* (p 204–225); the argument: character can be Fred or the explorer.
- *Behind the Vines* (p 342); Max is ill: character will be Lila.
- *Epilogue* (p 391–394); home: character can be Fred, Lila, Con, Max or the explorer.

T Ask more able children to be volunteers and come to the front, in role, as one of the characters. The rest of the class act as interviewers, asking questions as a group.

S Ask children to think about the character's personality in order to impersonate them.

D Ask children to focus on the way the character feels at the chosen point and how their personality is changing and developing with each new experience.

Starter activities 8–14

Group discussion: find a leader

Resources required: photocopy master (PCM) 1 (for reference only)

- **Children should be able to:**

  articulate and justify answers, arguments and opinions; consider and evaluate different viewpoints, attending to and building on the contributions of others; participate in discussions, presentations, performances, role play improvisations and debates.

1 Photocopy PCM 1 (the following pages give main character profile information: pages 29–30; 35–37; 145–149).
2 Divide the class into groups of four and explain that each group has to choose one of the three older children from the story (Con, Lila or Fred) to be their leader.
3 If groups are struggling, hand out the character summaries on PCM 1.
4 Ask one child in each group to feed back to the class, explaining their reasons.

This activity could be expanded into a main activity, by asking children to go into role as the character they have chosen as leader and to write or deliver an oral presentation on why they are the best candidate.

Starter activity 15

Using the senses

DURING READING

3 x   Vocabulary builder

- **Children should be able to:**

  give well-structured descriptions, explanations and narratives for different purposes, including for expressing feelings; participate in performances, role play and improvisations.

   infer characters' feelings, thoughts and motives.

1 Ask children to close their eyes and use their senses as they listen to the following scenes being read aloud.
   - *On the River* (p 167–169)
   - *Fishing in the Dark* (p 290–292)
   - *The Green Sky* (p 354–359)
2 Ask children to describe the sounds, smells, and what it looked and felt like to them.

D Ask children to select an evocative scene and read it expressively to a partner.

Starter activities 16–18

Debate

Children should be able to:

ask relevant questions to extend their understanding and knowledge; articulate and justify answers, arguments and opinions; give well-structured explanations for different purposes; maintain attention and participate actively in collaborative conversations; participate in discussions and debates; consider and evaluate different viewpoints, attend to and build on the contributions of others.

1 After reading the chapter *The Explorer*, explain that the class is going to debate two sides of the argument about the existence of the ruined city. One group represents promoting the city; the other keeping it a secret. Encourage everyone to participate.

2 Use the following prompts to facilitate discussion if needed.
   - Is it important to learn more about the world in which we live, even uninhabited regions?
   - If we know more about species under threat, are we better able to support and protect them?
   - What is the biggest threat to the Amazon? What damage can explorers do?
   - What has European involvement in the Amazon done to the region?
   - How are indigenous people often treated by newcomers?

Starter activity 19

Symbolism

Children should be able to:

ask relevant questions to extend their understanding and knowledge; articulate and justify answers, arguments and opinions; give well-structured explanations for different purposes; maintain attention and participate actively in collaborative conversations; participate in discussions and debates; consider and evaluate different viewpoints, attending to and building on the contributions of others.

reflect on spiritual, moral, social and cultural issues, using imagination to understand other people's experiences.

1 After reading the chapter *The Vow*, ask the class to think about how the tattoo binds all the children together forever.

2 Ask children to think of any other markings or symbols that people tattoo on themselves to symbolise beliefs or to belonging to a group or culture.

3 Encourage children to discuss the tattoos: the negative and positive impact on the person and others; their purpose; how they serve as a form of identification.

This activity works well with Main activity 13.

Starter activity 20

Job interview

- **Children should be able to:**

   ask relevant questions to extend their understanding and knowledge; give well-structured descriptions, explanations and narratives for different purposes; maintain attention and participate actively in collaborative conversations; participate in performances, role play and improvisations; select and use appropriate registers for effective communication.

   infer characters' feelings, thoughts and motives

1 After reading the chapter *A Note on Explorers*, ask children to imagine how the characters may have used their experience in the jungle for future job interviews.

2 Divide the class into pairs: one as the interviewer and one as the character (Lila, Fred, Con or Max). Explain they are going to do an imaginary job interview. Ask:

- What strengths and transferable skills did your experience give you?
- How did your experience change you? Was there a point when you felt ready to give up and what made you persevere?
- What quality is most valuable in a person, and why?

This activity works well with Plenary activity 18.

Starter activity 21

Freeze!

- **Children should be able to:**

  give well-structured descriptions, explanations and narratives for different purposes, including for expressing feelings; participate in performances, role play and improvisations; articulate and justify answers and opinions.

1 Divide the class into groups of four or five. Explain that each group has to choose a significant scene from the book and create a still scene for the rest of the class.

2 Ask each group to come up and perform their still scene at the front of the class. Ask the class to try to guess the scene that each group creates.

3 Once the scene has been guessed correctly, ask children to explain why they chose to represent it, what it means to them and why it is particularly significant.

Starter activity 22

Book review

- **Children should be able to:**

  give well-structured descriptions, explanations and narratives for different purposes, including for expressing feelings; participate in discussions; articulate and justify answers and opinions.

1 Ask children to choose their favourite part of the book and then to make their choice more specific: choose a scene, a conversation between characters or a single sentence.

2 Ask children to explain to the class why they have chosen their favourite part. This can be done as formally or informally as you like. They will need to justify why they've chosen it and what it means to them.

 Ask children to choose their favourite character and give five reasons why they like them.

Ask children to express how their favourite section of the book makes them feel and be aware that it doesn't have to make them feel good. It can be powerful in other ways, making them feel sad, moved, disgusted, etc.

This activity could be extended and turned into a main writing activity, with the book reviews displayed around the classroom.

Starter activity 23

Charades

- **Children should be able to:**

  participate in performances, role play and improvisations.

1 Write down some key scenes on separate pieces of paper, or use these:
   - *Flight* and *The Green Dark* (p 1–17); the crash
   - *The Monkeys and the Bees* (p 114–138); finding the honey and the map
   - *Smoke* (p 150–162); the fire
   - *At the Top of the Cliff* and *The Ruined City* (p 178–203); meeting the explorer
   - *Max* (p 334–340); Max becoming ill
   - *Flight Home* (p 378–388); the flight home.

2 In groups of three or four, ask children to play charades, acting out the key scenes. One member from each team picks a scene from a hat / bowl. (Fold the pieces of paper up so that the contents are hidden.)

3 Allow children to act out the scene, assigning roles and miming actions to the class. Ask the class to guess the scene.

Ask children to practise their scene before acting it out.

Starter activity 24

Hollywood pitch

- **Children should be able to:**

  give well-structured explanations for different purposes, including for expressing feelings; participate in discussions and debates; articulate and justify answers and opinions; consider and evaluate different viewpoints.

1 Put children in groups of four to six, to work on a short pitch for the film rights of *The Explorer* to Hollywood.

2 Explain the pitches need to be delivered orally and that children can make notes. Ask:
   - Why would the book make a great film?
   - Which elements of the book are particularly engaging cinematically?
   - Which elements of the book might need to be left out or adapted?
   - What music might be used, where could it be filmed and who might star in it?

3 Ask each group to come up in turn and present their pitch to the rest of the class.

Starter activity 25

17

Amazon animals

 Resources required: photocopy master (PCM) 8

- **Children should be able to:**

  give well-structured explanations for different purposes; participate in discussions and debates; articulate and justify answers and opinions; consider and evaluate different viewpoints.

1. Photocopy PCM 8 and cut out the individual Amazon animal cards, so that every child has their own set of cards.
2. Explain that these animals are all mentioned in the book, along with information about them and the risks they pose.
3. Ask children to number the animals from 1 to 10 in order of the danger they pose to humans, with 1 being the least dangerous and 10 being the most dangerous.
4. It's important that each child allocates the same number to each animal (for a future game that will be played), therefore everyone in the class needs to be involved in the discussion that decides and agrees the animal classification.
5. You could write the animals on the board: caiman; goliath tarantula; common tarantula, mosquito, bullet ant, vampire bat, maggot, piranha, caracara, panther.

The class should discuss and agree its decisions.

Starter activity 26

Pok-a-tok

 Resources required: basketball, walled playing field / sports hall

- **Children should be able to:**

  play competitive games, modified where appropriate; take part in outdoor and adventurous activity challenges.

   learn about Mayan civilisation.

1. Set up a playing court outside or in the hall. Draw chalk circles on the wall at each end of the court, or stick circles drawn on paper to opposite walls.

   Explain to children that the whole class is going to play a simplified version of the traditional Mayan game, pok-a-tok. Pok-a-tok is similar to basketball, with the aim of hitting the target at either end of a court. However, in pok-a-tok, participants can only use their fists, elbows or bottoms to bounce the ball against a wall and through the circle! If the ball falls to the floor, bounce it for the class so that the game can continue.

2. Divide the class into two teams and begin the game.
3. The winning team is the one that gets the highest number of hoop goals.

This could be played frequently as a starter or plenary to transition into / from breaktime.

Starter activity 27

Amazon animal showdown!

⏱ (15) **Resources required:** photocopy masters (PCM) 8 and 9, children's numbered cards from Starter activity 6

- **Children should be able to:**
  - participate in performances, role play and improvisations.
  - play competitive games.

1 Using the numbered cards from Starter activity 26, play a game of Amazon animal showdown.

2 Divide the class into groups of four and ensure every child in each group has a set of the already numbered Amazon animal cards and a copy of PCM 9 game rules.

3 Ask children to read the rules in pairs on PCM 9 or read them together as a class.

4 Children play the game in their groups of four.

(T) Ask children to work in pairs within their groups.

This game could be played frequently as a starter, or a plenary. It should be carried out after Starter activity 26.

— **Starter activity 28**

Guest list

 ⏱ (5)

- **Children should be able to:**
  - articulate and justify opinions; give well-structured explanations for different purposes, including for expressing feelings; participate in discussions and debates.

1 Ask the class to imagine that they're inviting some people over for dinner and that they have one space left.

2 Ask children in turn: who, out of the five characters in the book, they would choose to fill the last space.

3 Encourage children to explain their answers, thinking specifically about what their chosen guest would bring to dinner in terms of their personality.

(T) Ask children to work in pairs or small groups to come up with some ideas.

(D) Ask children to try to express how they think their chosen character would make other guests feel and what sort of company they would be.

— **Starter activity 29**

19

Poetry: vocabulary

 Vocabulary builder **Resources required:** photocopy master (PCM) 10; thesauruses

- **Children should be able to:**

  identify the audience for and purpose of the writing; select appropriate grammar and vocabulary.

1 Display or copy the poem on PCM 10 and read it together as a class.

2 Divide the class into pairs based on Pinpoint level. Ask the pairs to look at the following words from the poem and replace them with synonyms that are as evocative and imaginative. Children could use a thesaurus to find new words.

T Children working at 'towards level' can use this list:
- angry (stanza 1)
- beautiful (stanza 2)
- wishing (stanza 2)
- quickly (stanza 3)
- leaping (stanza 4)

S Children working at 'securing level' can use this list:
- noble (stanza 2)
- wise (stanza 2)
- deeds (stanza 2)
- rocket (stanza 4)
- splendid (stanza 4)

D Children working at 'deeper level' can use this list:
- sit (stanza 2)
- merely (stanza 2)
- uttered (stanza 3)
- jabber (stanza 3)
- swings (stanza 4)

3 Ask children to read through the poems, inserting their new words. Which version do they prefer?

Children could try writing their own verses of poetry using their alternative words.

Starter activity 30

Main activities

After the plane crash

⏱ 40

- **Children should be able to:**
  - ✏️ write for a range of real purposes; select appropriate grammar and vocabulary; describe settings, character, atmosphere; integrate dialogue in narratives.
  - **SPaG** use adverbials of time, place and number; use modal verbs.
  - 📖 identify how language, structure and presentation contribute to meaning; infer characters' feelings, thoughts and motives.

1. Choose a line from page 12 to inspire class writing and write it on the board. Explain that children are going to write an alternative version of events, starting with this prompt. Encourage children to use adverbials of time, place and number.

2. Encourage children to think about what the characters could have done following the plane crash, had they not run away. How will their narratives differ from the end of the chapter *The Green Dark* and *The Den*? Explain that 'could' is a modal verb. Explore other modal verbs, and how they can affect degrees of possibility in a piece of writing.

3. Ask children to replicate the style, tone and characters of the book. They don't need to conclude their narratives, just think of events for one chapter at a time. Children should give their chapter(s) their own title(s).

T Ask children to work in groups to come up with a plot idea and then write sections of the chapter each, which can then be compiled.

S Ask children to write at least one chapter, making sure that the characteristics of all of the characters are consistent with the original.

D Ask children to focus on how characters feel.

You could choose one of the chapters above for children to write an alternative ending for, based on your progress in the book so far, or you could allow them to choose once you have read all three. Alternatively, you could extend this activity over several sessions and look at all three chapters.

Main activity 1

Raft building mini-project

Resources required: suggested equipment: wood, polystyrene, plastic, glue, sticky tape, rope, string, nails, pins, 400 g weights or equivalent items, sink or other tank / tub filled with water

4 x 45

- **Children should be able to:**

  use research and develop design criteria to inform the design of innovative, functional, appealing products that are fit for purpose; select from and use a wider range of tools and equipment to perform practical tasks; evaluate their ideas and products; apply their understanding of how to strengthen, stiffen and reinforce more complex structures.

  identify 3-D shapes from 2-D representations; draw given angles; understand and use approximate equivalences between metric units and common imperial units.

  give reasons, based on evidence from comparative and fair tests, for the particular uses of everyday materials.

  articulate and justify answers, arguments and opinions; participate in presentations.

1. Once you've read the chapter *The Raft* (p 66–76), ask the class to design and build its own smaller raft, which must be able to float. Children will work in groups of four to design, build and test it.

2. All rafts should be the same dimensions: 12" by 6", one twelfth the size of the raft in the story. Ask the class to convert the dimensions to metric measurements (to the nearest centimetre) before starting. The raft should be able to support a weight of about 400 g.

3. In the first session of the mini-project, ask children to come up with a design for their raft and select their supplies. Supplies can be things that are available within school. Designs should be drawn in 3-D, showing the raft at different angles and including dimensions in cm. Supplies should be listed with details of quantities.

4. In the second and third sessions of the mini-project, ask children to build their rafts using their supplies. They should work as a team, using each other's skills and making sure that everyone is involved.

5. When the rafts are finished, explain that each raft will hold a 400 g weight to see whether they can successfully float. Place the rafts, loaded with their weights, in the water. Encourage children to check on their rafts at regular time intervals throughout the day and to make notes on their rafts.

6. In the final session of the mini-project, ask children to write up their findings as a group. Children should think about what made their raft float, or not, and what they might do differently next time.

7. Ask each group to present their project, explaining how they built their raft, whether it successfully stayed afloat and what they have learned.

Main activities 2–5

Alternative versions

- **Children should be able to:**

 write for a range of real purposes; select appropriate grammar and vocabulary; describe settings, character, atmosphere and integrate dialogue in narratives.

 use adverbials of time, place and number; use modal verbs.

 identify how language, structure and presentation contribute to meaning; infer characters' feelings, thoughts and motives.

1 Explain to the class that they're going to think up and write some alternative endings to some of the key chapters in the story, when the characters are at a decision crossroads.

2 Ask children to replicate the style, tone and characters of *The Explorer*. They don't need to conclude their narratives, just think of events for one chapter at a time. Children should give their chapter(s) their own title(s). Encourage children to use adverbials of place, number and time and add degrees of possibility to their writing with modal verbs.

The key themes for exploration are:

- **Leaving camp:** read the chapter *Smoke* to the end of page 158, when the characters are at a decision crossroads. Encourage the class to think about what the four children could have done had they not left camp on the raft during the fire.

- **Climbing the cliff:** read the chapter *At the Top of the Cliff* to the end of page 176, when the characters are at a decision crossroads. Encourage the class to think about what the characters could have done had they not climbed the cliff.

- **Choosing a pilot:** read the chapter *Behind the Vines* to the end of page 346, when the children have to decide which of them will fly the plane. Encourage the class to think about what might have happened had one of the other children volunteered to fly the plane, or if the explorer had, or if none of them had.

T Ask children to work in groups to come up with a plot idea and then write sections of the chapter each, which can then be compiled.

S Ask children to write at least one chapter, making sure that the characteristics of all of the characters are consistent with the original.

D Ask children to focus on how characters feel.

You could choose one of the chapters above for children to write an alternative ending for, based on your progress in the book so far, or you could allow them to choose once you have read all three. Alternatively, you could extend this activity over several sessions and look at all three chapters.

Main activity 6

Map making

 45

- **Children should be able to:**

   use fieldwork to observe, measure, record and present the human and physical features in the local area using a range of methods, including sketch maps, plans and graphs.

1 Having read the chapter about the map discovery, *The Monkeys and the Bees*, ask children to create their own maps. They could be maps of anywhere local: the route to school; their favourite place; a journey they do every day, etc.

2 Explain that the maps need to be accurate, drawn to scale as far as a possible, include plenty of detail and contain a key.

T Ask children to work in groups to develop a map together.

D Ask children to include as many geographical features on their maps as possible: footpaths; roads, parks; contour lines; buildings; a scale, etc.

Main activity 7

A letter home

50 **Resources required:** photocopy master (PCM) I (for reference only)

- **Children should be able to:**

   write for a range of real purposes; identify the audience for and purpose of the writing; select appropriate grammar and vocabulary; use a wide range of devices to build cohesion within and across paragraphs.

   link ideas using adverbials of time, place and number.

1 Explain that the children are going to write a letter home from the perspective of Con, Lila or Fred. They will need to think about the characters' relationship with their parent(s) or carer at home. Hand out PCM I for reference if needed.

2 Explain that children should try to use adverbials of time, place or number in their letters, where possible. Give examples on the board to support understanding.

T Ask children to write one letter about a specific event, explaining what happened.

S Ask children to write various letters, focusing on how their chosen character feels about what is happening and how they are affected.

D Ask children to write replies to their letters from the letter recipient, changing the perspective to reflect the recipient's personality.

Main activity 8

The explorer's diary

4 x ⏱45

- **Children should be able to:**
  - write for a range of real purposes; select appropriate grammar and vocabulary; use a wide range of devices to build cohesion.
  - infer characters' feelings, thoughts and motives.
  - use adverbials of time, place and number; use modal verbs.

1. Explain to the class that they are going to role-play as the explorer at key points in the story and write some diary entries from his perspective. They should think about: how he feels, what he thinks of the children, his plans, what he would like to happen and whether the company that has arrived is changing how he feels.

   - *The Ruined City* (p 186–203); meeting the children
   - *The Explorer* (p 204–225); a secret city
   - *Fishing in the Dark* (p 282–309); night fishing
   - *Waiting for Dawn* (p 366–376); saying goodbye

   T Ask children to focus on the events themselves, what happened, and when.

   D Ask children to focus on how the explorer feels when the children arrive.

Main activities 9–12

Design a tattoo

⏱40

- **Children should be able to:**
  - improve their mastery of art and design techniques.
  - write for a range of real purposes; select appropriate grammar and vocabulary.

1. Having read the chapter *The Vow*, explain to the class that they're each going to design their own tattoo that is a suitable reminder for the characters of their experience in the Amazon. The tattoo should represent what the jungle experience means to the four children and symbolise the secrecy. Remind the class that the tattoo will need to fit on Max's hand, be simple enough for the children to draw it and display its meaning clearly.

2. Ask children to sketch their designs before drawing the final version. Then ask them to write a small passage explaining how and why their tattoo is suitable.

   T Ask children to work in pairs or small groups to come up with a design together.

Main activity 13

My Amazon survival guide

 AFTER READING

- **Children should be able to:**

   write for a range of real purposes; use organisational and presentational devices to structure text [for example, headings, bullet points, underlining]; select appropriate grammar and vocabulary.

   use modal verbs to indicate degrees of possibility.

1 Explain that children are going to write their own guides for surviving in the Amazon jungle, based on what they have learned.

2 Encourage children to use headings to organise their guides. Here are some examples of headings they could use: Making a den; What to eat / What NOT to eat; Creating a map; How to build a raft; Survival top tips!

3 Encourage children to use modal verbs throughout their writing. Explore how modal verbs can contribute to meaning in their survival guides.

T Ask children to work in groups to compile a guide, with individuals writing the content for one of the headings, and then putting all the sections together.

D Ask children to use as many different writing styles as they can: instructions; labelled diagrams; non-narrative; narrative, etc.

Main activity 14

A letter to each other

- **Children should be able to:**

   write for a range of real purposes; identify the audience for the writing; select appropriate grammar and vocabulary; use a wide range of devices to build cohesion.

   infer characters' feelings, thoughts and motives.

   use adverbials of time, place and number.

1 Explain to the class that they're going to write a letter from the perspective of one of the four characters (Con, Lila, Max or Fred) to one of the other characters (this could also be the explorer).

2 Ask children to write from the perspective of the characters as adults, using the epilogue at the end of the book to inform their letters. Things to think about include what the character is doing now, how they feel about their experience in the jungle and how they feel about the character they're writing to.

- The letter should feel like it's written from the perspective of the character. Encourage children to use adverbials of time, place and number.

- The letter should reference how the experience has shaped their life.

- The letter should fill in some of the missing years between the children's rescue and the present day, for instance: how their relationship with the letter recipient has developed; how they as a character have changed; what they took from the experience; what they struggled to get over, etc.

T Ask children to write one letter, from one character to another.

S Ask children to focus more on how the experience in the jungle affected them emotionally.

D Ask children to write replies to their letters from the letter recipient, changing the perspective to reflect the recipient's personality. They could even write a series of letters from one and the other. Alternatively, children could swap letters with each other and write each other's replies.

Main activity 15

Autobiography

- **Children should be able to:**

   write for a range of real purposes; select appropriate grammar and vocabulary; use a wide range of devices to build cohesion.

   infer characters' feelings, thoughts and motives.

   use adverbials of time, place and number; use modal verbs.

1 Explain to the class that they're going to write an extract from the autobiography of one of the following characters: Con, Lila or Fred.

2 The extract can be about any aspect of their jungle experience. Encourage children to use adverbials of time, place and number, and explore how using modal verbs can add degrees of possibility to their writing. Here are some key moments:

- the crash (p 1–17)
- finding the honey and the map (p 114–138)
- the fire (p 150–162)
- meeting the explorer (p 178–203)
- Max becoming ill (p 334–340)
- the flight home (p 378–388).

T Ask children to write one extract focusing on what happened during the event.

S Ask children to focus on how the event made the character feel. They could write about one event or a number of events.

D Ask children to choose one of the events and write an extract from a variety of the characters' autobiographies, changing the perspective.

Main activity 16

The Amazon under threat mini-project

3 x ⏱45 **Resources required:** art materials, recording equipment, access to the internet and / or books about the Amazon

- **Children should be able to:**

  ✏ write for a range of real purposes; select appropriate grammar and vocabulary; use organisational and presentational devices to structure text; use a wide range of devices to build cohesion.

  💬 articulate and justify answers, arguments and opinions; participate in presentations.

  📝 use modal verbs; use adverbials of time, place and number.

  📍 use maps to focus on South America, concentrating on its environmental regions, key physical and human characteristics, countries and major cities; use maps, atlases, globes and digital / computer mapping to locate countries and describe features studied.

  🦋 identify scientific evidence that has been used to support or refute ideas or arguments.

1. After reading *A Note on Explorers* at the end of the book, explain to the class that they're going to work on a mini-project to research and write a report on how, and why, the Amazon is under threat.

2. Explain that the report could include artwork, sculpture, posters, an audio-visual presentation or advert to help convey the information.

3. Divide the class into groups of five and write the following headings on the board.

   - The history of the rainforest
   - The indigenous people of the Amazon
   - European invasion
   - Deforestation and climate change
   - Endangered wildlife

4. Explain that each group member needs to choose one of the headings to research, so that all of the topics are covered.

5. In the first session of the mini-project, children begin researching their heading, paying particular attention to statistics that they want to include in their report.

6. In the second session, children begin writing up their research findings, concentrating on cause and consequence of the long-term effect on the rainforest.

7. In the final session, groups compile their reports. They share what they learned about their topic and together work on a list of *'How to help'* suggestions.

8. Once the reports are finished, the class can present its findings to other classes or their parents in the form of an awareness campaign. Children should include surprising statistics and ways in which everyone can support the Amazon.

Ⓣ Ask children to work in pairs on one of the headings.

Ⓓ Ask children to include other representations of information, such as graphs.

Main activities 17–19

Amazon cookbook

- **Children should be able to:**

   write for a range of real purposes; select appropriate grammar and vocabulary; use a wide range of devices to build cohesion.

   use adverbials of time, place and number.

   improve their mastery of art and design techniques.

1 Divide the class into groups of four and explain that they're going to write their own cookbook, focusing on resources available in the Amazon.

2 Explain that each child will have their own recipe to write. They must cover the foods mentioned in the book and can combine ingredients in any way. This list of food may be useful to have on the board:

cocoa pods and beans; grubs; chocolate pancakes; pineapples; honey; figs; caracara; mangos; rats; armadillos; berries; tarantulas; sugar cane; coconut milk; piranha; acestrorhynchus (needle jaw fish); traira (wolf fish); caiman.

3 Encourage children to include meat, fish and vegetarian recipes as well as drinks. They should write where and how to find the ingredients as well as how to prepare and cook them. Encourage children to use adverbials of time, place and number.

4 The instructions for each recipe should be accompanied by illustrations.

🅣 Ask children to work in pairs or small groups to write and draw a recipe together.

Illustrated recipes may be displayed around the classroom.

Main activity 20

True or false?

- **Children should be able to:**
  - write for a range of real purposes; select appropriate grammar and vocabulary.
  - explain and discuss their understanding of what they have read.

1 Divide the class into groups of three or four. Explain that each group is going to write a true or false quiz, based on facts they have learned about the Amazon jungle. For example: bees can't see the colour red (true).

2 Ask each group to come up with a minimum of 12 facts: some true and some false.

3 Every quiz should be designed with two columns of boxes beside each statement, under the headings *True* and *False*.

Quizzes are used in Plenary activity 21. Write the answers down separately!

Main activity 21

A prequel

- **Children should be able to:**
  - write for a range of real purposes; select appropriate grammar and vocabulary; describe settings, character and atmosphere and integrate dialogue in narratives; use a wide range of devices to build cohesion.
  - use adverbials of time, place and number; use modal verbs.

1 Explain to the class that they're going to write the first chapter of a prequel to *The Explorer*, which tells the explorer's story.

2 Encourage children to think carefully about the character, the setting and the time. They could write about the explorer's life in the ruined city before he is discovered, his mission into the Amazon and plane crash, or further back to his life with a family.

3 Explore how using modal verbs can add degrees of possibility to the children's writing and encourage them to use adverbials of time, place and number where possible.

T Ask children to create a storyboard for the chapter, drawing images with captions to tell the narrative sequence.

D Ask children to write more chapters, trying to capture what has made the explorer the way he is in the book, what events may have changed him and why.

You may wish to extend this activity over more than one session.

Main activity 22

The Mayans mini-project

3 x (45) **Resources required:** recording equipment, access to the internet and / or books about Mayan civilisation

- **Children should be able to:**

 write for a range of real purposes; select appropriate grammar and vocabulary; use organisational and presentational devices to structure text; use a wide range of devices to build cohesion.

 use modal verbs; use adverbials of time, place and number.

 use maps to focus on South America, concentrating on its environmental regions, key physical and human characteristics, countries and major cities.

 learn about Mayan civilisation.

 articulate and justify answers, arguments and opinions; participate in presentations.

1. After reading *A Note on Explorers* at the end of the book, explain to the class that they're going to work on a mini-project to research and write a report on the Mayan civilisation.

2. Divide the class into groups of between four and six, and suggest that they divide the topics for their report amongst themselves. Children can choose their own Mayan topics to research and write about, or if they need any prompts, the following ideas could be used as chapter headings:

   - The rise of the Mayans
   - Mayan cities
   - Mayan food and drink
   - Royalty and power among the Mayans
   - The fall of the Mayans
   - Mayan artefacts – what's left behind?
   - Rediscovery
   - Mayan beliefs

3. In the first session of the mini-project, ask children to begin researching their topic.

4. In the second session, ask children to begin writing up their reports, remembering to support facts with evidence wherever possible. Explore how using modal verbs can add degrees of possibility to the children's writing and encourage them to use adverbials of time, place and number where possible.

5. In the final session, ask groups come back together to compile their reports, sharing what they learned about their topic with each other.

6. Once the reports are finished, ask each group to talk to the rest of the class about the most interesting thing they learned about the Mayans, and whether it made them feel any differently about the book and particularly the explorer himself.

T Ask children to work in pairs on one of the headings.

D Ask children to include other representations of information, as well as narrative, such as graphs and charts.

Main activities 23–25

My exploration mini-project

2 x ⏱(45) **Resources required:** recording equipment, access to the internet and / or books on South America

- **Children should be able to:**

  ✏ write for a range of real purposes; select appropriate grammar and vocabulary; use organisational and presentational devices to structure text; use a wide range of devices to build cohesion.

  📝 use modal verbs; use adverbials of time, place and number; use organisational and presentational devices to structure text [for example, headings, bullet points, underlining]

  🌍 use maps to focus on South America, concentrating on its environmental regions, key physical and human characteristics, countries and major cities; use maps, atlases, globes and digital / computer mapping to locate countries and describe features studied.

  💬 articulate and justify answers, arguments and opinions; participate in presentations; use spoken language to develop understanding through speculating, hypothesising, imagining and exploring ideas.

1 Explain to the class that they are going to think of somewhere they'd like to travel to or explore within South America.

2 Explain that once children have decided on their destination, they are going to create a travel documentary or travel brochure about their chosen area. Ask children to work independently or in a group if they share similar interests.

3 Ask children to think about the tone of their piece – is it going to be serious or more humorous? Explore how using modal verbs can add degrees of possibility to the children's writing and encourage them to use adverbials of time, place and number where possible.

4 In the first session of the mini-project, ask children to start researching their destination, using the following headings as a guide:
   - The environmental region
   - Key physical and human characteristics
   - Major cities; population, housing, industry, etc.
   - The people and the language
   - Climate
   - Why and when they would go, what they would do there and what is needed as essential survival kit for the environment.

5 In the second session, ask children to finish their travel pieces. If there is time, share the pieces in class. Otherwise, display them around the classroom or in the class library.

   D Ask children to include other representations of information, such as graphs and charts. There should be inclusion of statistical analysis for a more in-depth study.

Main activities 26–27

Inform the public

Resources required: current news articles about a dramatic event, including articles from children's publications

- **Children should be able to:**

 identify the audience for and purpose of the writing; select appropriate vocabulary; use organisational and presentational devices to structure text and to guide the reader.

 use expanded noun phrases for description and specification; use modal verbs.

1. Explain that children will write their own newspaper report about an aspect of the book, such as the plane crash, the missing children or the homecoming.

2. Look together at some of the newspaper articles, asking children how informative they are, how dramatic, whether they seem biased or objective, as well as what effect any organisational features have, such as headings, quotes, images, etc.

3. Ask children to think about the angle they want to present and what effect they want to have on readers. Encourage children to use expanded noun phrases, and to use modal verbs where possibility may be needed.

4. Once finished, ask children to swap articles with each other, reading them and feeding back on some of the points discussed at the beginning of the lesson.

Children could draw or source images to include in their reports.

Main activity 28

Rules of the game

Resources required: a selection of board / card game instructions

- **Children should be able to:**

 identify the audience for and purpose of the writing; select appropriate vocabulary; use organisational and presentational devices to structure text and to guide the reader.

1. Explain that children will write instructions for their own game. The game could be for the characters in the story to play, or be based on the book's jungle theme.

2. Hand out the instructions for existing games and look together at the features: how the text is organised; how instructions are made clear; how they are structured.

3. Once children have written their instructions, divide the class into groups of four or five to read each other's instructions to test how clear and coherent they are.

Ask children to work on their instructions in pairs or small groups.

As an extension or plenary activity, the class could create additional resources required for a game, and play it, using the instructions to test out efficacy.

Main activity 29

Poetry: performances

Resources required: photocopy masters (PCM) 10, 11 and 12; filming equipment

- **Children should be able to:**

 identify the audience for and purpose of the writing; select appropriate vocabulary; use organisational and presentational devices to structure text and to guide the reader.

 continue to read and discuss an increasingly wide range of poetry; prepare poems to read aloud and to perform; ask questions to improve their understanding; summarise main ideas and identify key details that support the main ideas; check that the book makes sense and discuss understanding.

 participate in performances.

1. Divide the class into groups of three or four and explain that they are going to look at some poems about the jungle.

2. Hand out the poems to the groups and explain that each group is going to prepare a performance of their poem.

3. Explain that groups need to work together to develop their understanding of the poem and that each member of the group should take on a role to help their analysis of the poem, e.g. summariser, questioner and clarifier.

    - **Summariser:** identifies the main points of a text and puts the information into their own words
    - **Questioner:** uses closed questions to check understanding and open questions to explore the poem further
    - **Clarifier:** identifies problems with the poem and seeks clarification

4. Encourage children to think about intonation, tone and volume as well as how they read aloud as a group: are they all reading or are some group members acting elements out; are some adding sound effects, music, etc?

T Ask children to work on *Road-Song of the Bandar-log* (PCM 10).

S Ask children to work on *Letting in the Jungle* (PCM 11).

D Ask children to work on *The Law of the Jungle* (PCM 12).

As an extension activity, you could film the groups performing their poems.

Main activity 30

Plenary activities

Fronted adverbials

 Resources required: Photocopy master (PCM) 2

- **Children should be able to:**

  select appropriate grammar and vocabulary, understanding how such choices can change and enhance meaning; use a wide range of devices to build cohesion within and across paragraphs.

READ UP TO PAGE 7

1 Photocopy PCM 2 and distribute it to the class.

2 Explain that fronted adverbials are used to link sentences and paragraphs. Adverbials of time express when something happened (*later, next, before*), where something happened (*nearby, under, by*) and the order in which things happened (*firstly, secondly*).

3 Ask children to add fronted adverbials to each of the sentences on the PCM. These can be adverbials of time, place or number.

You could write examples of adverbials on the board to help. Remind children about adding a comma after fronted adverbials.

— **Plenary activity 1**

Brazilian food review

 Resources required: sample restaurant and recipe reviews (only)

- **Children should be able to:**

  select appropriate grammar and vocabulary; use organisational and presentational devices to structure text and to guide the reader.

   use expanded noun phrases.

   articulate and justify answers and opinions.

DURING READING

1 Explain that children can review any Brazilian food that they have tried or can imagine, and write reviews of meals that the characters in the book eat.

2 Explain that children need to think about how a dish looks, smells and tastes. They could rate the dishes, explaining why they have given each score.

3 Once the reviews are finished, ask children to compare what they thought about the different foods, discussing similarities and differences.

4 Explain that children are going to put their pieces together in a 'Brazilian Food' magazine. Encourage children to find images and recipes online for the dishes or to create their own.

 Ask children to look at some example restaurant and recipe reviews.

This activity would work well with the Starter activity 2.

— **Plenary activity 2**

Descriptive phrases

Vocabulary builder

- **Children should be able to:**
  - select appropriate vocabulary.
  - use relevant strategies to build their vocabulary.
  - expand noun phrases by the addition of modifying adjectives, nouns and preposition phrases.

1 Look together at the chapter *Maiden Voyage*, specifically Con's description of the birds in the Amazon as compared to those at home (p 83).

2 Explain that describing the birds as doing something that they wouldn't ever do, such as going for a job interview, is a good way to create a powerful image.

3 Explain to children that they are going to write some powerful descriptive phrases of their own. The phrases should be about everyday things, brought to life using unusual and powerful comparisons. Remind them that the phrases don't have to be positive as long as they're evocative.

Encourage the use of expanded noun phrases. The structure below might help as a starting point.

- *The [blank] are like [blank], e.g. The park was like a desolate desert – windswept and constant, as far as the eye could see.*

— Plenary activity 3 —

Word of the day

Vocabulary builder

- **Children should be able to:**
  - select appropriate vocabulary.
  - use relevant strategies to build their vocabulary.

1 As you read the book, stop at intervals and ask children to choose a word or phrase from the recent chapters that they weren't familiar with before reading.

2 Ask children what they think their word might mean, and encourage them to then use a dictionary to look up the correct definition.

3 Once children understand their word, explain that they are going to write a sentence of their own using it. This can be done at various times throughout the reading.

Children could keep a vocabulary book, noting new words for future reference.

— Plenary activity 4 —

Sequencing

3 x

- **Children should be able to:**

  participate in discussions and debates.

  check that the text makes sense.

DURING READING

1. At three points during the book, divide the class into groups of three or four and explain that children should put the events listed from the story into the correct order in which they happened.

2. Write the events (in the order they're written here) on the board. The correct order is in brackets.

Sequencing 1: read to page 176
- Con opens up about her childhood. (6)
- The children find a sardine tin. (4)
- Fred says goodbye to his watch. (2)
- Fred discovers pineapples. (5)
- Lila makes chocolate pancakes – sort of. (3)
- The first sighting of Piranhas in the river. (1)

Sequencing 2: read to page 315
- The explorer takes the children night fishing. (5)
- The children eat tarantulas. (3)
- The children make their vow. (7)
- The children make supper for the explorer. (4)
- The children sneak a look behind the vines. (1)
- Fred sets his first trap. (2)
- The explorer saves the children from a caiman. (6)

Sequencing 3: after reading
- Max gets ill. (3)
- The explorer tells the children about vampire bats. (1)
- Con decides to stay. (6)
- The children play stuck in the mud. (2)
- The children see the plane. (4)
- Fred lands the plane in the ruined city. (5)

Ask children to write a short summary about each of the events.

Plenary activities 5–7

Vocabulary quiz — DURING READING

3 x Vocabulary builder **Resources required:** photocopy masters (PCM) 3, 4 and 5

- **Children should be able to:**
  - explain the meaning of words in context.
  - use relevant strategies to build their vocabulary.

1. At three points during reading, explain that the class is going to play a quiz, using some of the unusual vocabulary. It can be played as a class or in pairs.
2. Photocopy the following.
   - PCM 3 (for vocabulary quiz 1 after pages 29–200)
   - PCM 4 (for vocabulary quiz 2 after pages 328–331)
   - PCM 5 (for vocabulary quiz 3 after pages 367–375)

   As you read out each question, children guess the word that it is describing.

 Write the answers on the board in a random order, so that children just have to match the correct word to the definition. Alternatively, write the first letter of each answer on the board instead.

Plenary activities 8–10

Instructions — READ UP TO PAGE 138

- **Children should be able to:**
  - select appropriate grammar and vocabulary; use organisational and presentational devices to structure text and to guide the reader; assess the effectiveness of their own and others' writing.
  - use adverbials of time, place and number; use modal verbs.

1. Once you've read the chapter, *The Monkeys and the Bees*, explain to the class that they're going to write some instructions for directions to a place.
2. Explain to children that they need to think about a particular journey they do by foot (it should be quite a short journey), such as their walk to school.
3. Explain that children should write a set of clear, written instructions (no images) on how to make the journey, how the person using the instructions would know they're on the right route (e.g. particular landmarks) and how long it should take. They should think about features to use to make the instructions clear, such as numbered lists and bullet points, and how to avoid creating long passages of narrative.
4. Ask children to swap instructions and say whether they are clear enough.

Plenary activity 11

Family descriptions

 Vocabulary builder

- **Children should be able to:**

   select appropriate vocabulary.

   use relevant strategies to build their vocabulary.

1 Look together at the chapter *Fishing in the Dark*, specifically where Fred describes his father at home (p 304).

2 Ask children to discuss the image that the description creates in their minds of Fred's father, and how the language does this.

3 Ask the class to write some descriptive sentences about one of their own family members. This can be someone that children are close to or not, someone they know a lot about or very little. They should think about something that person does, the impression they give and how their personality makes the children feel. The phrase should be non-literal and use metaphors and similes. Examples:

- My mum came in the front door, wrapped in a warm smile.
- The emptiness of her life followed her into every room.
- The sofa was warm, but sitting next to him I could feel a constant breeze of cold air and whistling wind on my skin.

Plenary activity 12

Stuck in the mud

- **Children should be able to:**

   play competitive games.

1 Once you've read the chapter *Stuck in the Mud*, explain that the class is going to play the game.

2 Take the class outside if possible, or otherwise to a hall, and explain the rules:

- One child starts off being *it*, chasing the others in order to tag them.
- Once children have been tagged, they need to freeze.
- Tagged children have to stay frozen until an untagged child crawls through their legs, which frees them.

This game could be played frequently as a starter or plenary.

Plenary activity 13

A memory

READ UP TO PAGE 333

- **Children should be able to:**
  - identify the audience for and purpose of the writing; select appropriate vocabulary.
  - listen and respond appropriately to adults and their peers; articulate and justify opinions; use relevant strategies to build their vocabulary.
  - use relative clauses beginning with *who, which, where, when, whose, that*, or an omitted relative pronoun.

1. Look together at the end of the chapter *Stuck in the Mud*, where Fred reflects on the experience of playing stuck in the mud during a storm. He talks about how the memory stays with him, years on, like a 'gold coin'.

2. Ask children to share with the class something that they have done that has stayed with them. They should explain why it holds significance and how it plays a role in their life now.

3. Encourage children to compare their memory with something and explain the comparison. Children can write memories down if they wish.

Plenary activity 14

Metaphors

READ UP TO PAGE 373

 Vocabulary builder

- **Children should be able to:**
  - select appropriate vocabulary.

  use relevant strategies to build their vocabulary.

1. Look together at the chapter *Waiting for Dawn*, specifically the conversation between Con and the explorer, where the explorer explains to Con how her face has given her away (p 373).

2. Ask children to discuss the metaphor and what image it creates of Con and how she's feeling.

3. Explain that children are now going to write some descriptive phrases using metaphors that help to create pictures in their readers' minds.

   Some examples to help might be:
   - *His leg was a crumpled piece of paper.*
   - *Her heart stung.*
   - *The grief streamed past him in a torrent of water.*

Plenary activity 15

Bravery

READ UP TO PAGE 381

- **Children should be able to:**

  listen and respond appropriately to their peers; give well-structured explanations for different purposes, including for expressing feelings.

1 Read the advice that the explorer gives the children as they board the plane to return home from the jungle at the end of the book. He refers to their extraordinary bravery and how the world is waiting to be impressed by it.

2 Divide the class into pairs, and ask children to talk to each other about something they've done that was brave. It doesn't have to be adventurous, it can be overcoming a fear, finding resilience and strength at a difficult time, or just being out of their comfort zone and doing something new.

3 Once children have had about five minutes to do this, ask pairs to come to the front of the class and explain what their partner did that was brave and what they thought of their bravery.

Plenary activity 16

Exploring definition

READ UP TO PAGE 388

Vocabulary builder

- **Children should be able to:**

  select appropriate vocabulary.

  explain the meaning of words in context.

  use relevant strategies to build their vocabulary.

1 At the very end of the book, the author gives two definitions of what the word 'exploring' could mean. Look at the two alternatives and ask the class why they both might be right, and which one is more accurate to them.

2 Ask children to come up with their own definition (one or two sentences) of the word 'exploring', encouraging them to write it formally, as if in a dictionary.

3 Once children have written their definitions, encourage volunteers to read them out and see how many alternatives you get.

T Ask children to work in pairs on their definition.

D Ask children to write an antonym for 'exploring'.

Definitions could be displayed around the classroom.

Plenary activity 17

42

CV

Resources required: photocopy master (PCM) 6

- **Children should be able to:**
  select appropriate grammar and vocabulary; use organisational and presentational devices to structure text.

1. Photocopy PCM 6 and hand out to each child.
2. Once you've read the epilogue, which sees the characters 12 years on, ask the class to think about the jobs that all the children have now got and how they relate to their jungle experience.
3. Explain to the class that they are going to imagine themselves as one of the children at the point that they're applying for their job. They should think specifically about: the character's strengths; the skills they developed in the jungle; the impact of the jungle experience.
4. Ask children to fill in the CV template (PCM 6) for one of the children characters.

D Ask children to write an accompanying covering letter to go with the CV, expressing more personally the skills and strengths they feel they have.

This activity works well as preparation for Starter activity 21.

Plenary activity 18

Character summary

Resources required: photocopy master (PCM) 1 (reference only)

- **Children should be able to:**
   write for a range of real purposes; select appropriate grammar and vocabulary; use a wide range of devices to build cohesion.
   use expanded noun phrases; use modal verbs.

1. Photocopy PCM 1 and hand it out to children.
2. Explain that children are going to write their own character summary to add to the ones on the PCM, about themselves.
3. Explain that the summary should be 80–100 words. It should be an honest summary of their character, which includes traits that children believe serve them well and ones that they feel hold them back.
4. Encourage children to think specifically about how they would manage, excel or struggle in an extreme situation such as being stranded in the Amazon.

Children could illustrate their descriptions with relevant artworks.

Plenary activity 19

Film rights

- **Children should be able to:**
  give well-structured explanations for different purposes, including for expressing feelings; participate in discussions and debates; articulate and justify answers and opinions; consider and evaluate different viewpoints.

1 Divide the class into groups of six and explain that they are actors / actresses that have just been cast in the film version of *The Explorer*.

2 Ask children to divide up the roles of the six characters and decide who would be best to play each one, and why. Children should also think about which character(s) they are least suitable to play, and why.

3 Bring the class back together and ask for a summary from each group.

Ask children to express what they would offer the role, how they would play it and why they're suitable.

This activity would work well with Starter activity 25.

Plenary activity 20

True or false?

Resources required: children's true or false quizzes from Main activity 21

- **Children should be able to:**

   participate in discussions and debates.

   distinguish between statements of fact and opinion; explain and discuss their understanding of what is read to them.

   play competitive games.

1 Explain to the class that they're going to play a game using the true or false quizzes that they wrote in Main activity 21.

2 Divide the class into groups of four and hand out a quiz to each group (ensuring that it's unknown to the whole group).

3 Ask one child from each group to be the quizmaster, with the others being the contestants. The contestants need to work as a team to decide true or false.

4 Once all the questions have been asked, ask the quizmaster to write the total scores on the board. Circulate the roles within each group, using a new quiz each time.

This activity should be carried out after Main activity 21. The class could create and answer quizzes on other aspects of the book: character quizzes, plot quizzes or even vocabulary quizzes, such as those in Plenary activities 8–10.

Plenary activity 21

The sequel

- **Children should be able to:**

  select appropriate vocabulary; describe settings, characters and atmosphere and integrate dialogue; use a wide range of devices to build cohesion.

  use expanded noun phrases; use modal verbs; use relative clauses.

  infer characters' feelings, thoughts and motives; predict what might happen from details stated and implied.

1 Explain that the class is going to write the plan for a sequel to *The Explorer*.
2 Explain that the sequels can focus on any of the characters they met in *The Explorer*, or all of them, as well as introducing new characters.
3 Ask children to include where and when their story will start (e.g. straight after where we leave the characters, or a few years down the line) and what the premise will be (e.g. another exploration; a rescue mission, etc.) in their plans.
4 Explain that the sequel plans should have a clear starting point, plot climax and ending. Children also need to give their sequels a title.

T Ask children to draw a storyboard for their sequel, instead of a written plan.

If there is time, children could think about powerful opening lines. This activity could be developed into a main activity in which children begin to write their sequels.

Plenary activity 22

Read all about it

 Resources required: current newspaper articles about dramatic events that have good headlines and taglines

- **Children should be able to:**

 identify the audience for and purpose of the writing; select appropriate vocabulary; use organisational and presentational devices to structure text and to guide the reader.

use expanded noun phrases; use modal verbs.

1. Cut out the headlines and taglines from the newspaper articles, and display.

2. Look at the newspaper headlines and taglines together and ask children to give their reactions to them, thinking specifically about: their effect and impact; how they make children feel; whether they make them want to read the whole article; how much information they give and how dramatic they are.

3. Divide the class into pairs and explain that children are going to create some headlines and taglines that sum up and inform people about the children's experience in the jungle.

4. Ask the pairs to present any element(s) of the story that they choose in their headlines, thinking about how important, interesting and engaging the event is to the wider public and from what angle they want to present it. Headlines should be no more than ten words, taglines could be up to 30 words.

Plenary activity 23

Animal fact file

 Resources required: access to the internet / books on Amazon wildlife

- **Children should be able to:**

write for a range of real purposes; use organisational and presentational devices to structure text and to guide the reader.

1. Explain that the class is going to create an animal fact file, in groups or pairs, for one of the animals in the book (e.g. caiman, tarantula, mosquito, etc.).

2. Ask children to choose one of the animals and to make notes on what they already know about the animal. They can do some extra research if they need to.

3. Explain that their fact files should include: name; habitat; size / weight; key characteristics (shy, aggressive, friendly, deadly); diet (meat eater, vegetarian).

4. Explain that children can draw or print off an image of the animal to add detail.

Ask children to create fact files for a number of different animals from the book, doing additional research to include statistics and figures.

Plenary activity 24

School reports

2 x ⏱(10) **Resources required:** photocopy master (PCM) 7

- **Children should be able to:**

 identify the audience for and purpose of the writing; select appropriate vocabulary; use organisational and presentational devices to structure text and to guide the reader.

 use expanded noun phrases; use modal verbs.

1 Photocopy PCM 7 and hand out two copies to each child.

2 Explain to the class that they are going to choose one of the characters from the book about whom to write two school reports: one during this lesson and another at the end of the next lesson. The first report will be from before the plane crash and the other from after the children have returned home.

3 Explain that children need to write into PCM 7 using the headings to guide them.

4 For the first report, explain that children should think about: what the character was like at the very beginning of the book; what they were confident and unconfident in; what skills they had; how resilient they were emotionally; their relationships with their family members and how they felt about themselves.

5 For the second report, explain that children should focus on: how the character has changed and developed; what skills or strengths they may have picked up (practical and emotional); how they may have struggled to fit back into school life; the skills they developed in the jungle and the impact of the jungle experience.

T Ask children to focus on events that have happened.

S Ask children to focus on the emotional changes and development.

D Ask children to write a report from a parent or guardian in response to the school report: one from before the jungle experience and one from after, detailing how the character behaves and has changed at home.

Plenary activities 25–26

Poetry: write a poem

 Vocabulary builder **Resources required:** photocopy master (PCM) 10 (only)

- **Children should be able to:**
  - identify the audience for and purpose of the writing; select appropriate grammar and vocabulary.
  - prepare poems to read aloud and to perform.

1 Explain to the class that they're going to write their own short poem about *The Explorer*, and that the poem can be written about, or in response to, any element of the book: an event; a character; a friendship; an animal; a sight or sound, etc.

2 Explain to the class that poems don't have to rhyme, but they should be evocative and powerful in representing something from the book.

3 Children could read their poems out once they're finished.

 Ask children to look at PCM 10 for support.

Plenary activity 27

Record a trailer

 Resources required: recording equipment

- **Children should be able to:**
  - articulate and justify opinions; give well-structured descriptions and narratives for different purposes, including for expressing feelings; participate in discussions, performances, role play, improvisations and debates.

1 Divide the class into groups of four, and explain to children that they will be recording a radio trailer for the book.

2 Explain that each group needs to write its own trailer, which should be no more than 350 words, summing up the premise of the book, introducing the key characters and giving enough of a taste of what's to come without giving too much away.

3 Ask children to put some thought into what else would make the trailer enticing, such as sound effects, voices, music, etc.

4 Ask the groups to use the recording equipment to record their trailer.

5 Play the recordings back to the class and ask children to vote on the most effective one.

S Ask children to express what makes the trailers effective or not, and whether they'd entice children to read the book.

D Ask children to explain how trailers could be changed or adapted to increase effect.

Plenary activity 28

The UK vs the Amazon rainforest

- **Children should be able to:**
  - listen and respond appropriately to their peers; articulate and justify answers, arguments and opinions; consider and evaluate different viewpoints, attending to and building on the contributions of others.
  - note and develop initial ideas, drawing on reading and research where necessary.
  - understand geographical similarities and differences through studying human and physical geography of a small area of the United Kingdom and a region within South America.

1. Divide the class into pairs and explain that each pair is going to draw up a comparison list to compare the United Kingdom with the Amazon.
2. Ask children to draw a line down the middle of a piece of paper to create two columns, one column should be headed *The United Kingdom* and the other *The Amazon*.
3. Explain that pairs need to think of as many things as they can that are different between the two regions. Some things to think about are: climate; wildlife; mountains; rivers; population; landscape, etc.

D Ask children list similarities and differences between the UK and the Amazon.

Plenary activity 29

Character development

- **Children should be able to:**
  - listen and respond appropriately to their peers; articulate and justify answers, arguments and opinions; consider and evaluate different viewpoints, attending to and building on the contributions of others.
  - select appropriate grammar and vocabulary.

1. Divide the class into pairs and explain that each pair is going to draw up a before and after list of the characteristics for each character, which shows how that character has changed and developed by the end of the story.
2. Encourage pairs to think as much as possible about how the experience in the jungle and the influence of the other characters impacts the character, thinking specifically about what they go on to do in later life.

Plenary activity 30

Character summaries

PCM 1

Con

Con is an orphan living with her great-aunt, who didn't really want her. Every summer, Con is sent away to a convent school. She has travelled a lot, and has a photographic memory. She is brave and very determined, but can be a bit bad-tempered and people often think she is rude. She is sometimes pessimistic and suspicious, which makes her a little cautious. Con has a real strength of character, so once she gives something a go, she usually succeeds at it.

Fred

Fred lives in England with his dad, who works a lot and doesn't have much time for him, so Fred goes to boarding school. He's tall for his age and mature, which makes him seem older than he really is. He is calm under pressure, makes decisions carefully and is very capable. Fred can be proud, so will often do things even if others tell him not to, which makes him quite independent. Fred is also kind and thoughtful and works well in a team.

Lila

Lila lives in Brazil with her mama and papa, who are scientists. She is clever and kind, as well as maternal: perhaps because she is used to looking after her younger brother, Max. She knows a lot about the natural world from her parents, and she is more familiar than the others with Brazil and the plants and animals that live there. Lila is not as confident as the others and doesn't push herself to do things she's not comfortable with, but is always positive and optimistic. Lila is a great team player.

Fronted adverbials

Add fronted adverbials to each of the sentences below.

_____ we built a den.

_____ and because it was getting dark, we lit a fire.

_____ we found some wood we could burn.

_____ we decided to build a raft.

_____ we gathered branches we could tie together.

_____ we found some vines we could use as ropes.

_____ we tested it on the water.

_____ we needed to gather some food and other supplies.

_____ we set off.

_____ we could see the city.

> Remember, fronted adverbials are always followed by a comma. They can show time, place or number.

Vocabulary quiz 1

PCM 3

Use pages 29–200 of the book to answer these questions.

1. What are you if you are very thirsty and in need of water?

   _____

2. What is the name of a large hole filled with human waste and dirty water? _____

3. What is the name of a South American reptile, similar to a crocodile or an alligator? _____

4. What is the name of a fierce, predatory South American fish that has very sharp teeth? _____

5. What is the name of a slow-moving South American mammal that hangs upside down from trees? _____

6. What is the name of an expert in the study of plants?

   _____

7. What is the name of a large South American bird of prey? _____

8. What are the highest branches of the trees in a forest called?

   _____

9. What is something called if it is active at night? _____

Vocabulary quiz 2

PCM 4

Use the book to answer these questions.

> You'll find all these words on pages 328–331.

1. Which word describes the way sunlight comes into a space slowly through a small opening?

   _____

2. Which word describes a situation that seems hopeless and dismal (it is also a word to describe cold, harsh weather)?

   _____

3. If you skin has become tough and hardened, what would it be?

   _____

4. If you don't trust something or someone, what are you?

   _____

5. Which word describes people who don't like being criticised or challenged? _____

6. What action involves suddenly thrusting your body forward?

   _____

7. If you do something in a way that isn't smooth or graceful, how might you be doing it? _____

8. If the expression on someone's face is intense or deep, what is it?

   _____

9. If words are used in their usual sense without any exaggeration, what are they? _____

Vocabulary quiz 3

PCM 5

Use the book to answer these questions.

1. What is the name of the instrument that shows the direction of north and south?_____

2. What is the name of a rounded roof?_____

3. What is the name for someone who is unconventional or strange? _____

4. If someone is rude and arrogant, what are they?_____

5. What word means the same as uncomplimentary or unfavourable? _____

6. If someone lacks courage and is scared of everything, what are they? _____

7. What is another word for mad?_____

8. If someone does something very systematically, how are they doing it?_____

9. What is a wide street called?_____

10. What is another word for undoubtedly or unquestionably?_____

You'll find all these words on pages 367–375.

CV template

PCM 6

Name: _____

Strengths: _____

_____

_____

_____

Skills: _____

_____

_____

_____

My biggest challenge: _____

_____

_____

_____

What motivates me: _____

_____

_____

School report template

Name:_____

Strongest subject:_____

Subject to work on:_____

Biggest contribution to the classroom:_____

_____

_____

Areas to develop:_____

_____

_____

Relationships with other class members:_____

_____

_____

Behaviour:_____

_____

_____

Strengths outside the classroom:_____

_____

Amazon animals

PCM 8

Caiman

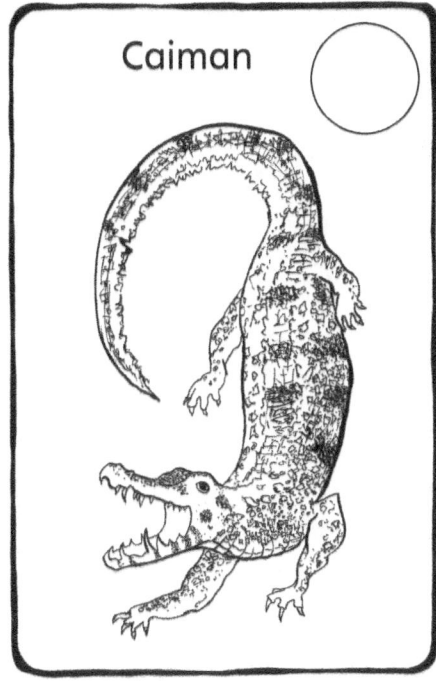

Goliath tarantula

Bullet ant

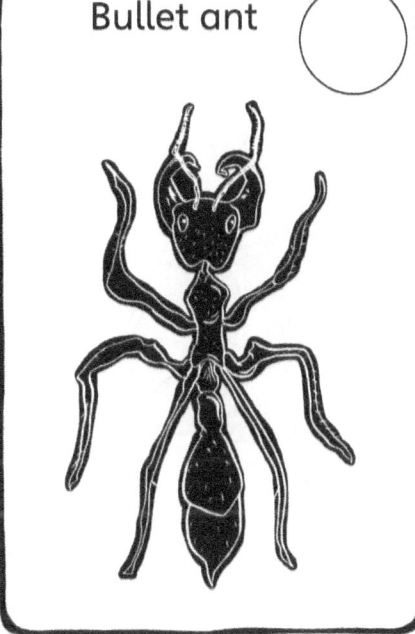

Common tarantula

Mosquito

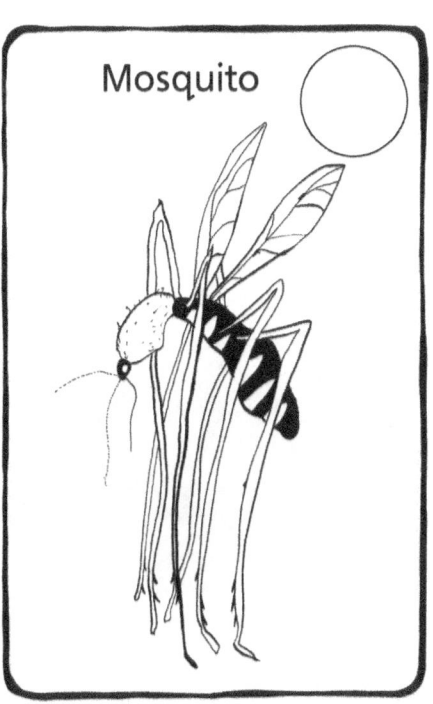

Amazon animals (continued)

PCM 8

Vampire bat

Maggot

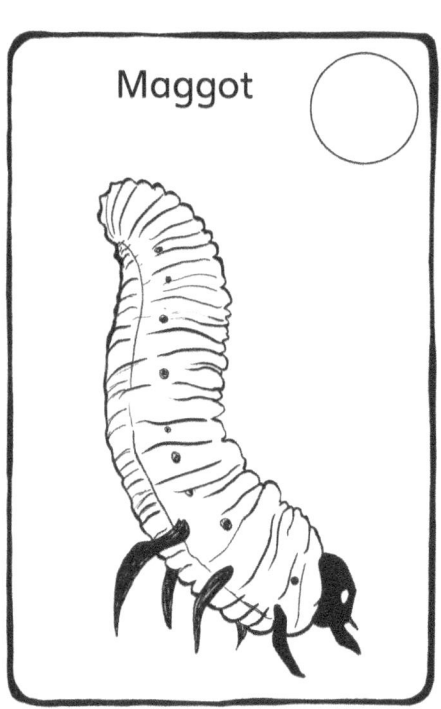

Panther

Piranha

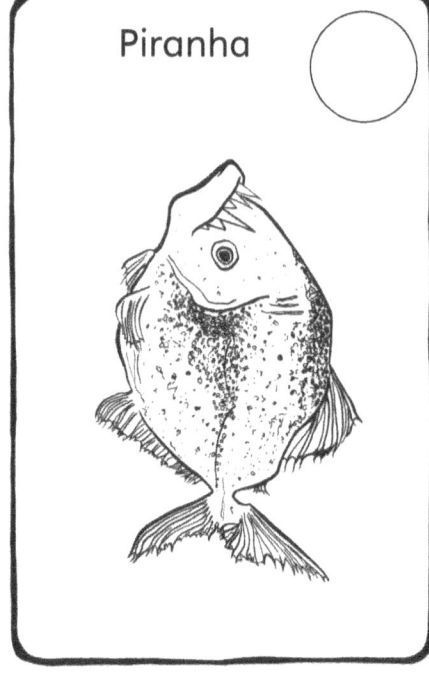

Caracara

Amazon animal showdown!   PCM 9

- Each player gets a set of the ten animals. They shuffle them and lay them out, animal face up, one by one in two rows of five.

- Players take 30 seconds to memorise the position of the animals and then turn their cards over.

- The player with the most recent birthday goes first, by turning over a card of their choice and placing it in the middle of the table.

- Play moves clockwise around the table, with each child choosing and placing a card.

- Whoever places the most-deadly animals wins the battle and takes all the cards in the pile, placing it beside them on the table.

- The winner then goes first in the next round.

- Children need to think tactically, because if very deadly animals have already been placed, it might be better to use a less-deadly animal and save the more-deadly ones for rounds with a better chance of winning.

- The aim is to have the most animal cards at the end.

- If children place the same animal down in the middle, a showdown begins, with children taking their next card simultaneously and placing them in the middle (such as in snap), so no tactics can be used.

- If children are left with any unplayed cards, these are added to their pile of wins.

Road-Song of the Bandar-log

Here we go in a flung festoon,
Half-way up to the jealous moon!
Don't you envy our pranceful bands?
Don't you wish you had extra hands?
Wouldn't you like if your tails were — so —
Curved in the shape of a Cupid's bow?
    Now you're angry, but — never mind,
    Brother, thy tail hangs down behind!

Here we sit in a branchy row,
Thinking of beautiful things we know;
Dreaming of deeds that we mean to do,
All complete, in a minute or two —
Something noble and wise and good,
Done by merely wishing we could.
    We've forgotten, but — never mind,
    Brother, thy tail hangs down behind!

All the talk we ever have heard
Uttered by bat or beast or bird —
Hide or fin or scale or feather —
Jabber it quickly and all together!
Excellent! Wonderful! Once again!
Now we are talking just like men!
    Let's pretend we are ... never mind,
    Brother, thy tail hangs down behind!
    This is the way of the Monkey-kind.

Then join our leaping lines that scumfish through the pines,
That rocket by where, light and high, the wild grape swings.
By the rubbish in our wake, and the noble noise we make,
Be sure, be sure, we're going to do some splendid things!

Rudyard Kipling

Letting in the Jungle

Veil them, cover them, wall them round—
Blossom, and creeper, and weed—
Let us forget the sight and the sound,
The smell and the touch of the breed!

Fat black ash by the altar-stone,
Here is the white-foot rain
And the does bring forth in the unsown,
And none shall affright them again;
And the blind walls crumble, unknown, o'erthrown
And none shall inhabit again!

Rudyard Kipling

The Law of the Jungle

Now this is the Law of the Jungle—as old and as true as the sky;
And the Wolf that shall keep it may prosper, but the Wolf that shall break it must die.

As the creeper that girdles the tree-trunk the Law runneth forward and back—
For the strength of the Pack is the Wolf, and the strength of the Wolf is the Pack.

Wash daily from nose-tip to tail-tip; drink deeply, but never too deep;
And remember the night is for hunting, and forget the day is for sleep.

The jackal may follow the Tiger, but, Cub, when thy whiskers are grown,
Remember the Wolf is a hunter—go forth and get food of thine own.

Keep peace with the Lords of the Jungle—the Tiger, the Panther, the Bear;
And trouble not Hathi the Silent, and mock not the Boar in his lair.

When Pack meets with Pack in the Jungle, and neither will go from the trail,
Lie down till the leaders have spoken—it may be fair words shall prevail.

When ye fight with a Wolf of the Pack, ye must fight him alone and afar,
Lest others take part in the quarrel, and the Pack be diminished by war.

The Lair of the Wolf is his refuge, and where he has made him his home,
Not even the Head Wolf may enter, not even the Council may come.

The Lair of the Wolf is his refuge, but where he has digged it too plain,
The Council shall send him a message, and so he shall change it again.

If ye kill before midnight, be silent, and wake not the woods with your bay,
Lest ye frighten the deer from the crops, and the brothers go empty away.

The Law of the Jungle (continued)

Ye may kill for yourselves, and your mates, and your cubs as they need, and ye can;
But kill not for pleasure of killing, and SEVEN TIMES NEVER KILL MAN.

If ye plunder his Kill from a weaker, devour not all in thy pride;
Pack-Right is the right of the meanest; so leave him the head and the hide.

The Kill of the Pack is the meat of the Pack. Ye must eat where it lies;
And no one may carry away of that meat to his lair, or he dies.

The Kill of the Wolf is the meat of the Wolf. He may do what he will,
But, till he has given permission, the Pack may not eat of that Kill.

Cub-Right is the right of the Yearling. From all of his Pack he may claim
Full-gorge when the killer has eaten; and none may refuse him the same.

Lair-Right is the right of the Mother. From all of her year she may claim
One haunch of each kill for her litter, and none may deny her the same.

Cave-Right is the right of the Father—to hunt by himself for his own.
He is freed of all calls to the Pack; he is judged by the Council alone.

Because of his age and his cunning, because of his gripe and his paw,
In all that the Law leaveth open, the word of the Head Wolf is Law.

Now these are the Laws of the Jungle, and many and mighty are they;
But the head and the hoof of the Law and the haunch and the hump is—
Obey!

Rudyard Kipling

Answers

PCM 3

1. dehydrated (p 37); 2. cesspool (p 37); 3. caiman (p 44); 4. piranha (p 47); 5. sloth (p 108); 6. botanist (p 29); 7. caracara (p 200); 8. canopy (p 132); 9. nocturnal (p 171)

PCM 4

1. filtered (p 328); 2. bleak (p 328); 3. calloused (p 329); 4. suspicious (p 329); 5. defensive (p 330); 6. lunge (p 330); 7. awkwardly (p 331); 8. vivid (p 331); 9. literal (p 331)

PCM 5

1. compass (p 367); 2. dome (p 367); 3. eccentric (p 368); 4. insolent (p 368); 5. unflattering (p 370); 6. coward (p 370); 7. insane (p 371); 8. methodically (p 372); 9. boulevard (p 372); 10. indubitably (p 374)